It was a quiet afternoon on the farm, when suddenly...

DUCK!

meg mcKinlay   Nathaniel Eckstrom

WALKER BOOKS
AND SUBSIDIARIES

It was a quiet afternoon on the farm. The horse was swishing his tail and the cow was chewing her cud. The pig was wallowing in the mud and the sheep was sheeping on the grass.

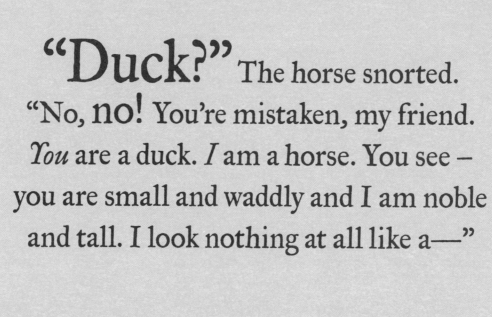

"Duck?" The horse snorted.
"No, no! You're mistaken, my friend.
You are a duck. *I* am a horse. You see –
you are small and waddly and I am noble
and tall. I look nothing at all like a—"

"DUCK!"

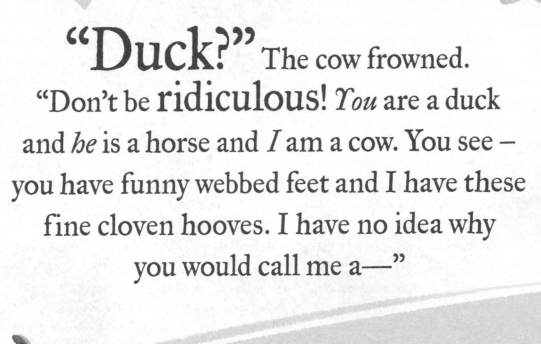

"Duck?" The cow frowned.
"Don't be **ridiculous!** *You* are a duck
and *he* is a horse and *I* am a cow. You see –
you have funny webbed feet and I have these
fine cloven hooves. I have no idea why
you would call me a—"

"Duck?" The pig squealed. "Please! *You* are a duck and *he* is a horse and *she* is a cow and *I* am a pig. You see – you have a poky little beak and I have a fine pink snout. Why on earth would you think I am a—"

"Duck?" The sheep scoffed. "Are you even **listening?** *You* are a duck and *he* is a horse and *she* is a cow and *he* is a pig and *I* am a sheep. You see – you have fluffy little feathers and I have a fine woolly coat. I have absolutely nothing in common with a—"

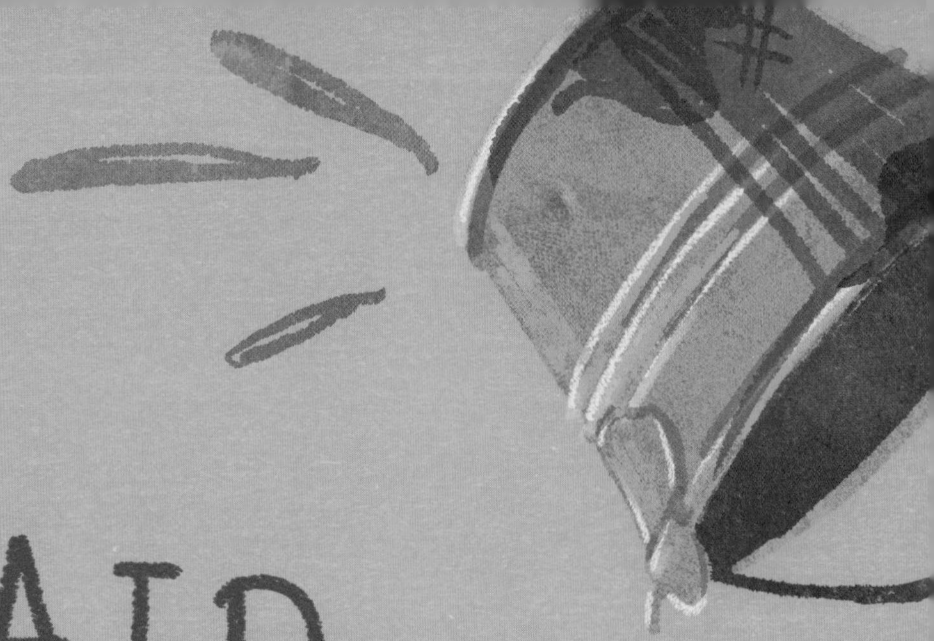

"I SAID DUCK!"

"Now **listen.**
You need to stop this nonsense
right **now.**"

"You have to understand
that everyone is different."

"Oh, you're right.
Quite right.
I do apologize.
I should never have said DUCK.

I should have said..."

For all the little folk who have
important things to say.
M.M.

For Brigham.
N.E.

First published in Great Britain 2019 by Walker Books Ltd
87 Vauxhall Walk, London SE11 5HJ

This edition published 2020

2 4 6 8 10 9 7 5 3 1

Text © 2018 Meg McKinlay
Illustrations © 2018 Nathaniel Eckstrom

The right of Meg McKinlay and Nathaniel Eckstrom to be identified as
the author and illustrator respectively of this work has been asserted by
them in accordance with the Copyright, Designs and Patents Act 1988

This book has been typeset in Historical

Printed in China

British Library Cataloguing in Publication Data:
a catalogue record for this book is available from the British Library

ISBN 978-1-4063-9472-6

www.walker.co.uk